PAWSITIVELY PERILOUS

SIT, STAY, SLEEP COZY MYSTERIES
BOOK 3

PATTI BENNING

SUMMER PRESCOTT BOOKS PUBLISHING

Copyright 2025 Summer Prescott Books

All Rights Reserved. No part of this publication nor any of the information herein may be quoted from, nor reproduced, in any form, including but not limited to: printing, scanning, photocopying, or any other printed, digital, or audio formats, without prior express written consent of the copyright holder.

**This book is a work of fiction. Any similarities to persons, living or dead, places of business, or situations past or present, is completely unintentional.

CHAPTER ONE

Sadie Barton had one million things on her to-do list, and every single one of them was urgent. Or, at least, that was how it felt. The world probably wouldn't end if she didn't change the garbage bag in the lobby right away, but it had only been a week since Sit, Stay, Sleep Motel and Boarding opened its doors to guests, and she was still trying to make sure everything went perfectly.

It was a losing battle.

"Excuse me?"

A guest called out to her as she passed through the lobby toward the laundry room, where freshly washed bedding for one of the dogs in the boarding kennels was waiting to be moved into the dryer. She paused, one foot propping the laundry room door open as she turned around.

"How can I help you?"

The nervous-looking middle-aged woman wrung her hands together. "Um, we're checking out. I left the key in the drop box, but I wanted to let you know little Benny threw up his breakfast on the carpet. I feel terrible, but we don't have time to clean it—"

"Don't worry about it," Sadie said, proud of the fact that her polite smile didn't slip for even an instant. "I hope he's feeling better. Did you have a good stay other than that? If so, we would really appreciate it if you could leave a good review."

"We had a very comfortable night. Thank you so much. I'll leave a review as soon as we get on the road."

Sadie waited until the woman left the lobby to slip into the laundry room. Instead of going for the washing machine, she made a beeline for the carpet cleaner and rags, already fighting her gag reflex. Cleaning up a mess made by a dog didn't faze her one bit, but when it came out of a human, even a little kid, it was a different matter entirely. She knew running a motel wasn't glamorous, but she wasn't sure she had been entirely prepared for the grimy reality of it.

She was tempted to tell Penny about the cleanup,

but her friend was already running herself ragged, trying to keep their guests happy. Even though Sadie's primary responsibility was the dog boarding and training half of their dog motel business, and Penny's was the running of the motel itself, they both needed to pitch in when and where they could. Building a sustainable business from the ground up with just the two of them was going to take all the hard work and cooperation they could manage.

If that meant Sadie had to scrub a kid's vomit out of their brand new carpet, darn it, she would do it. Maybe not with a smile on her face, but it would get done.

Ten minutes later, she was on her way back to the lobby, having propped Room Six's door open so it could air out. She passed Penny on the way—her friend was carrying two full garbage bags out to their brand new dumpster. Professional-grade garbage service wasn't cheap, but they couldn't keep just setting their bags out by the road. No one wanted to stay at a motel with a mountain of garbage bags outside.

They exchanged a nod, the most contact they'd had all morning. Both of them had been up since dawn—Sadie to take care of the dogs and clean the kennels like she did every morning, and Penny to begin the never-ending list of chores that kept the motel running. Sadie was pretty sure their washers and dryers hadn't stopped running once since they opened the rooms to guests.

After putting the cleaning supplies away, she finished moving the dog bedding from the washer into the dryer—they had two units of each, one of which was set aside specifically for the dogs—then returned to the lobby to check the motel's voicemail and email. Their rooms weren't exactly packed full, but they'd had a steady stream of business all week, which meant for the first time since buying the motel a month and a half ago, they were making money and not just losing it.

She was in the middle of typing a response to an email asking if they did discounted rates for long stays when the lobby door opened. She looked up, half expecting to see Penny, but instead saw a man she didn't recognize. He had the harried look of a traveler and was dragging a suitcase behind him. His button-up shirt looked well made, but it was sweat-stained, and his slacks were wrinkled. He made his way directly over to the desk and leaned against it as if exhausted.

"Please tell me you have a vacancy."

"Yes, sir, we do. Do you have a preference between pet and non-pet friendly rooms?"

"Whatever is cheapest," he said. "Can I pay with cash?"

"You can, but we require the entire payment up front. How long will you be staying?"

"I've got enough here for…" He reached into his pocket and pulled out his wallet, then counted the contents. "Three nights? Can I extend my stay later if I want to?"

"Absolutely," she said. "I'll just need your ID so I can finish checking you in."

He paused in the middle of counting his cash, his eyes flicking up to her face. "Actually, I was hoping to avoid that," he said. "I'm willing to pay a little extra if you'll forgo the ID check."

Warning bells rang in Sadie's mind. "I'm sorry, but our insurance requires that we check ID. I can't make an exception for anyone."

"Are there any places nearby that wouldn't ask for it?"

"If there are, then I'm not aware of them," she said. "From what I understand, it's a normal requirement these days."

His shoulders slumped. "Fine, just… if someone

calls or shows up looking for me, will you tell them I'm not here? It's important."

"We don't ever give out guest information without consent," she assured him.

He looked reassured and reluctantly slid his ID across the counter to her. She recorded his name, Martin Gleason, and his driver's license number, then handed it back to him and accepted the cash. After counting it out, she got a key from the organizer in the drawer under the register.

"I'm putting you in Room Ten," she said. "It's all the way down at the end. Check out is at eleven in the morning, and since you're all paid up, all you have to do is drop the key in the drop box. If you'd like to extend your stay, just call or stop in at the lobby whenever someone is here, and we'll get you taken care of."

"Thanks," he said as he took the key from her. "I appreciate it. You're a lifesaver."

She watched him go, then took out her phone to watch him on the security camera as he walked down the row of rooms toward the very last one. Wanting to pay in cash was normal enough, especially for the rural area around the tiny town of Greencreek, Georgia, but asking if she would rent him a room without seeing his ID was concerning. She couldn't think of a single good reason for someone to make that request. Either he was hiding from the law or he was hiding from someone else. Either way, it meant trouble.

While her eyes were on the camera, she spotted a familiar white delivery van turning into the parking lot. Their twice-weekly delivery of cookies from Sunshine Desserts had arrived. She exited out of the camera app and sent a quick text message to Penny to let her know to keep an eye on the guest in Room Ten. She would tell her the details later, but for now, they both needed to be on the lookout for any suspicious activity. The last thing they needed was to be caught up in a drug deal or some other sort of illegal activity.

She rose to her feet just as the lobby door opened. She had been expecting to see Bailey Tengu, the owner of Sunshine Desserts, but a young man she didn't recognize entered instead, his arms loaded high with boxes of cookies. The ones intended for dogs were marked clearly with permanent marker on all sides, along with cute little drawings of paw prints.

"Hey, there," he said, peering around the tower of boxes. "You've got a delivery. Where should I put these?"

"Right over here," she said. "Let me help you with that."

She helped him carry the boxes over to a locked cupboard in the back corner of the lobby, where an ancient tube TV and dead houseplant once stood. The cupboard was the best they could come up with for storage—they couldn't exactly keep the cookies in the laundry room right next to the cleaning supplies, and Sadie didn't want to have to trek up to her little apartment above the lobby whenever someone ordered one.

As much as she would have liked to offer cookies to their guests for free, they needed every penny they could get right now, and anything and everything from Sunshine Desserts was popular. The dog cookies were especially popular for her boarding clients. Almost every owner was happy to spend a few extra dollars on a cookie for their dog in hopes that it would brighten their stay.

So far, she had been able to find a flavor that each dog liked, and she made sure to take pictures of them eating the treat to send to their owners. In a lot of ways, their canine guests were easier to care for and keep happy than their human ones were.

"Thanks," Sadie said as the young man helped her stack the boxes inside the cupboard. "I don't think I've seen you around before. Did Bailey hire a new driver?"

"Yep," the young man said. He dusted off his hands and held one out to shake with her. "I'm Hunter Underwood. It's nice to meet you. Oh, she sent me an invoice, too. I think it's here somewhere…" He trailed off and patted his pockets until he finally withdrew a folded square of paper. Sadie accepted it, and Hunter paused to look around the lobby. "You know, I remember when old Mr. Bennington closed this place down. I didn't think someone would reopen it, not after all the murders that happened here. Your sign out front says you do boarding, too?"

Sadie, who winced at the word 'murders,' forced herself to nod. "We do boarding, and pretty soon I'll be offering dog training. Do you have a dog?"

"No, but my mom does. A little yorkie she babies. It's hard for her to travel because she never wants to leave the dog behind. Do you mind if I tell her about this place? She might want to pop in and have a tour and get a feel for it before she schedules something, but I know she has a cruise coming up she's been stressed about."

"Absolutely," Sadie said. "Tell her she's free to come by any time. There's usually someone in the office until around seven."

"All right," he said. "I can't promise anything, but

I know she'd rather board her yorkie somewhere local, and I think she'll like this place."

Before Sadie could respond, the lobby door opened again, this time to let Martin back in. He had a metal lockbox about the size of a standard notebook in his hands, and paused halfway across the floor when he saw Hunter. Hunter stared at him for a second, then brushed past him without another word.

Sadie raised her hand in a wave goodbye, then turned back to Martin, her smile feeling strained. Her list of things to do just kept growing. Where was Penny when she needed her?

CHAPTER TWO

"Hi, again," she said to Martin, trying to sound cheerful rather than stressed. "What can I help you with this time?"

"I forgot to ask, but do any of the rooms have a safe in them?"

She knew some hotels had safes in their rooms that guests could use for a price, but until they could afford to upgrade, the motel was about as basic as it got.

"I'm sorry, we don't," she said. "The credit union might offer safety deposit boxes, but I'm not sure if you have to be a member to use them."

"I don't know if I'll be here long enough for it to be worth setting something like that up." He hesitated, looking around the lobby, as if hoping a safe would jump out at him. "You don't have anywhere secure I could store this? I don't want to just leave it in my room unattended, but I can't bring it with me everywhere I go."

She hesitated. "What's in it?"

His grip on the lockbox tightened. "I'm sorry, but I don't think that's any of your business."

"I'm not trying to be nosy," she said. "I live above the lobby. I could store it in my apartment for you, if that would make you feel better, but I don't want to offer if it's something illegal like drugs or… I don't know, a gun or something."

"Oh." He looked relieved. "It's nothing like that. It's nothing that would get me in trouble with the law—it's just something I couldn't replace if it was stolen. Would you be willing to store it up there for me? Do you keep your door locked?"

"I do," Sadie said hesitantly. She regretted the offer already. "I don't think you have to worry about keeping it in your room, though. We have security cameras and we haven't had any issues with theft, and the only people going in to clean would be myself or Penny, the other owner."

"I'd feel more comfortable being able to store it elsewhere," he said. "Look, I'll pay you an extra hundred dollars if you'll keep it locked away upstairs and don't tell anyone it's here."

"I'm not sure—"

"An extra three hundred," he said. "Cash." He dug into his pocket and pulled out his wallet, withdrawing three crisp hundred-dollar bills.

She stared. Hadn't he emptied his wallet when he paid for the room earlier?

"I don't know if I'm comfortable with this."

"Look, I'll sign something stating it's nothing illegal and nothing dangerous. In fact, I'd like to have a written receipt from you, too, if that's okay."

He held the money out to her. She hesitated a second longer, but they did need the cash, and if they had a signed contract to protect them both, at least she would have plausible deniability if it did turn out to be something like drugs. She would have to store it out of Jasper's reach, just to be on the safe side.

"Let me type something up," she said, her shoulders slumping in defeat.

Five minutes later, she was making photocopies of a paper signed by both of them, which listed the terms of their contract. She would keep the lockbox safe without looking inside of it, and guaranteed that he would be able to get it back upon request. She had made him initial by a clause stating that he guaranteed the lockbox didn't hold anything illegal or dangerous.

"There you go," she said, handing his copy over to him. She slipped her own copy into the hidden bottom of the cash register, then quickly checked the bills for counterfeit.

"Are we all set?" Martin asked. "I shouldn't be here too long, but if it's more than a week or two, I might need to get something out of it."

"Just tell me whenever you want the box, and I'll get it for you," she said. She still didn't like it, but she thought she had done everything reasonable to protect herself, and the three-hundred dollars would help a lot.

"I appreciate this," he said as he left.

She watched him go, then grabbed the lockbox and carried it up to her apartment. She was burning with curiosity about what it held, but it didn't feel right snooping after she agreed not to, and she wasn't sure if she could open it anyway. It wasn't as if she knew how to pick locks.

She stashed it on a high shelf at the back of her closet and tried not to think about it too much as she went back downstairs, locking the door to the apartment behind her. The lobby door opened just as she returned to her spot behind the counter, and a newcomer came in. She knew as soon as she saw him that he was a tourist. He couldn't be anything else in his brightly colored button-up T-shirt, his cargo shorts, and the leather sandals he wore over his socks.

"Welcome," she said. "How can I help you?"

"I'd like a room if you can spare one," he said. "If not, I'd appreciate it if you can point me in the direction of another establishment as lovely as this one."

"You're in luck. We should be able to fit you in," she said, clicking to open their scheduling program on the computer. "How many nights will you be staying?"

"Let's start with three and go from there," he said. "I'm meandering my way on down to Florida, but I'm not in a hurry to get anywhere, and I like exploring little out-of-the-way towns like this. What do you need from me?"

"Just your ID and a card or cash," she said. "I'll put you in Room Six."

The carpet should be dry by now, and she knew it was ready for him because she had just cleaned it herself. He passed over his ID and a credit card, and she got him checked in. Paul Anderson, who according to his ID, was from all the way up in Boston.

"You're all set, Paul," she said, handing his cards back to him along with a key. "I hope you have a pleasant stay. Just pop in to the lobby if you need anything. Oh, and could I interest you in a cookie? We get them fresh from a lovely little dessert shop right here in town."

He was an easy mark and left a couple of minutes later, two cookies poorer. She tucked the cash away in the register and noted down the flavors he had taken. She and Bailey were trying to work out which cookies sold best at the motel. So far, the basics—chocolate chip, snickerdoodle, sugar cookies—were the most popular, but some of the more unique flavors were a hit, too.

She returned to the email she had been working on way back before Martin came in and typed two words. When the lobby door opened again, it was all she could do not to groan, but this time it was Penny who came through. She was carrying a bundle of bedding and rushed it through the lobby to the laundry room.

"You don't want to know," she called out over her shoulder. "Don't let anyone in Room Two. Give me five minutes to get this load started, then I'll take over from whatever you're doing. Thanks for handling things while I was busy."

The laundry room door swung shut behind her.

Sadie breathed a sigh of relief and quickly finished typing the email before hitting send.

Running the motel would take effort from both of them, but there was a reason her dream had always been to open her own kennel and training business. She would rather work with dogs than people any day.

CHAPTER THREE

Sadie was in the middle of trying to convince an elderly bulldog to take his medication—a feat that was easier said than done since he seemed to have a supernatural ability to sense the pill no matter where she hid it—when Penny peeked into the kennels from the laundry room.

"I've got someone in the lobby who says her son said you'd give her a tour of the kennels if she came in today. Her name is Tiffany Underwood."

"Oh, that's right," Sadie said. "Her son is Hunter, he's the new delivery driver for Sunshine Desserts. He mentioned something about her stopping in, but I didn't expect it to be this soon. Can you tell her I'll be right out?"

When Penny left, she turned back to the bulldog

and placed her hands on her hips. "All right, buddy. I've tried this the easy way, but now we have to do it the hard way. I promised your mom I'd make sure you got your medication every day, and I can't let her or you down. Sorry about this."

She held a dog treat carefully between her lips as she pried his jaws open and shoved the pill to the back of his throat. She held his mouth shut as she quickly retrieved the dog treat and held it in front of his muzzle temptingly. She waited until his tongue darted out to poach the treat before she released his jaws and let him eat it. She watched him for a second to make sure he didn't cough the pill back up, then gave a sigh of relief and backed out of the kennel, where she checked his dose of medication off on the care sheet that was pinned next to his kennel.

She stopped off in the laundry room to scrub her hands in the wash basin, then entered the lobby to find a put-together middle-aged woman sitting in one of the uncomfortable waiting chairs. She rose to her feet as Sadie approached.

"Hi, are you Tiffany?"

"I am, and you're Sadie, right?"

"That's me." They shook hands, and Sadie added, "It's nice to meet you. Hunter said you have a yorkie that you might be interested in boarding here?"

"Yes, sweet little Petunia," she said. "She's eight years old, and I've never boarded her before. She's tiny, and I hate the thought of leaving her with anyone, but my sister and I want to take our mother on a cruise next month. She's always wanted to go, and she's getting up there in age, so this might be our only chance. I've been beside myself trying to figure out what to do with Petunia. Hunter offered to watch her, but I just don't know. Don't get me wrong, he's a wonderful boy, but he's not always the most responsible."

"Well, I'm happy to give you a tour of the kennels," Sadie said. "And if you want to bring Petunia in for a test day and leave her for a few hours during the day or overnight to see how she does, you're welcome to do so. I live in the apartment above the lobby, so I'm here almost all the time, and each kennel has a security camera in it so I can check the dogs remotely. Here, follow me and I'll show you our setup."

She showed Tiffany their kennels, then brought her around to the back to show her the outdoor runs so she could see for herself that they were secure, even for a small dog. By the time they returned to the lobby, she could tell Tiffany felt a lot better about the prospect of boarding Petunia.

"I had my doubts. I know the reputation of this place, but I also know it's under new ownership now. I almost turned around when I pulled into the parking lot and saw the exact same vehicle my ex-husband used to drive—I figured it might be a bad omen. But the kennels look lovely and clean, and you seem responsible. I'd like to schedule something to see whether Petunia likes being here before I commit to boarding her for the full two weeks."

"Of course," Sadie said. "We'll just need her vet records. You can either print them out and bring them in or ask the clinic to email them to us. What day works best for you?"

They ended up scheduling an overnight stay for Petunia in two days, on Saturday, with the understanding that Sadie would call Tiffany if she thought Petunia was too stressed and needed to be picked up early. Sadie took down Tiffany's information, then walked her to the door. It felt good to be able to help someone who was nervous about boarding their dog. She knew firsthand how tough it could be to find someone she trusted with Jasper, and she hoped her place could be a comfortable place for Petunia to stay —and maybe give Tiffany a little more freedom to travel.

Evenings at the motel tended to be quieter than

mornings, since most of their guests checked out before noon and that was when they cleaned the rooms. With Penny keeping an eye on things in the lobby, Sadie had time to care for the dogs. Each of them got a long walk through the ten acres of Georgia forest they owned behind the motel before she fed them dinner.

They didn't get much foot traffic in the lobby after seven, which meant she felt comfortable taking Jasper out of his kennel to let him hang out with her in the lobby while she cleaned.

She was in the middle of sweeping the floor when she spotted something on the counter next to Penny's laptop: a little paper bag from Sunshine Desserts that was stapled shut, with the name Martin Gleason written on the front in permanent marker. He must have called the lobby to ask for one, except Penny had forgotten to bring it to him.

"Wait here for me, buddy," she said to Jasper, who was happily chewing on a rubber ball stuffed with treats on his bed in the corner of the lobby.

She didn't always let him hang out with her in there during the day in case a guest brought an unfriendly dog in, but she liked to have him with her during the quieter times, and she knew he liked to be involved in whatever she was doing. He didn't seem to mind his kennel, but she knew he would rather be with her if he had the choice.

She grabbed the paper bag with the cookie in it and stepped outside. The temperature had started to drop a little as the sun went down, but she could feel the heat emanating from the asphalt and wondered, not for the first time if they shouldn't paint it white to try to keep the temperature down. She hated the thought of it burning a dog's feet when their owner had to walk them from the car into the building.

She knocked on the door to Room Ten heard the click of a deadbolt and the slide of a chain before Martin opened the door.

"Yes?" he said. "Did someone come looking for me?"

"No," she said. "I'm just bringing you your cookie." She offered the bag to him.

He leaned out and took it from her. "Oh, thank you. I appreciate it. You're sure no one strange has been by?"

"I've got no reason to lie to you," she said. "Is there someone in particular I should be looking out for?"

"I don't know. I'm probably just being paranoid," he said. "Thanks again for the cookie."

He shut the door in her face, and she heard the

deadbolt engage as she turned away. She knew their tiny little roadside motel was bound to attract some shady characters, but she wasn't sure what to make of Martin. He seemed harmless, but she didn't like the fact that she had his lockbox hidden in her apartment or that he seemed so worried someone was going to come looking for him.

They'd had already been through enough. They didn't need any more trouble.

CHAPTER FOUR

Sadie had been wanting to open her own boarding and training business for as long as she could remember. She had been lucky enough to spend the past few years working for a successful commercial kennel, so she could see how it was run and get experience training a variety of dogs. While she had enjoyed that job and had been grateful to work somewhere she could bring Jasper with her every day, in the weeks and months prior to purchasing the motel she had felt as if she was outgrowing the place. She was as prepared as she could get…or so she thought.

There had been one consequence of owning her own boarding business that she hadn't been prepared for—and that was the fact that she might never get to sleep late again. With other people's dogs under their care, she couldn't slack off. She put them out for the last time at ten each night, then shut the barriers between the indoor and outdoor runs so the wildlife couldn't bother them while she was asleep, and she had to be up by seven to let them out each morning.

Maybe one day, she and Penny would have reliable employees who could take care of the early mornings and late nights for them, but for the foreseeable future, sleeping in later than seven was a thing of the past.

At least the dogs didn't care what she was wearing. She spent the early hours of the next morning in her pajamas while she checked the dogs and let them outside, then in her scrubs while she cleaned kennels and prepared their breakfasts. It wasn't glamorous, but it was comfortable, and she couldn't complain about being greeted by their happy, furry faces first thing in the morning.

Penny was the one who had it worse, in her opinion—while Sadie was feeding dogs and cleaning kennels, her friend was dealing with early checkouts and cleaning motel rooms.

It was mid-morning by the time Sadie finished all of her daily kennel chores. She stopped in the lobby to see how Penny was holding up before she went upstairs to get changed, Jasper following at her heels.

Penny was at the front desk on the phone, but when she saw Sadie, she muted the call and said, "Hey, have you seen or heard from the guy in Room Ten this morning? I need to see if he wants cleaning service or not. I knocked and called, but he didn't answer. His car's still here, though."

"No, I haven't," Sadie said. She felt a twinge of concern. "He's the one who asked me to store that lock box for him, and he was worried that someone was going to come look for him. I hope it was all just in his head."

Her friend frowned. "Do you think something happened to him?"

"I don't know. It might be worth checking on him, just in case."

"Let's go together. Give me two seconds to get off this call."

While she waited for Penny, Sadie brought Jasper up to her apartment above the lobby and, just to be on the safe side, grabbed her pepper spray, which she shoved into her pocket alongside her cell phone and the spare key for Room Ten. She double-checked the lockbox while she was at it. She regretted agreeing to keep it, but she wasn't sure how to go back on their agreement now.

Penny hadn't been thrilled when Sadie told her

about the deal, but she admitted she probably would have done the same thing. They needed the money, and as long as they weren't doing anything that was outright illegal or harmful, they couldn't turn down three hundred dollars. It was as simple as that.

Penny was waiting for her when she came downstairs. They stepped out of the lobby and headed down the row of rooms together. Not even half of their rooms were full—Rooms One, Six, and Ten had guests in them, and they had a reservation for Room Four tomorrow night, but they weren't exactly bursting at the seams. She hoped that would change with time, though, for now, she was just grateful they were getting any business at all.

Penny shot her a worried look when they reached Room Ten. Sadie was the one who stepped forward and knocked on the door.

"Mr. Gleason," she called out. "Would you like cleaning service?"

There was no response. She tried knocking again, but still nothing. Glancing around the parking lot, she spotted his vehicle—an older SUV—still parked in the same spot it had been in the day before. Her stomach soured. He hadn't put up the Do Not Disturb sign, and technically they reserved the right to enter any of the rooms at any time, but knowing how paranoid he was, it still felt wrong to go in when he might be there.

But if he *was* there, why wouldn't he answer their knock? Something was wrong.

"I'm going to open the door," she decided.

"Be careful," Penny said. "I don't like this at all, Sadie. He has to be in there. His car's still here. There's nowhere else he could be."

"Maybe he took a walk," Sadie murmured, though she didn't believe her words any more than Penny seemed to.

She slipped the key into the lock and disengaged the deadbolt, then knocked one more time before pushing the door open.

Martin had all the lights off and had pulled the blinds shut. The air conditioning was cranked to max, but as far as Sadie was concerned, that was normal. She always did the same when she stayed in a hotel. The air conditioning units cost them an arm and a leg in electricity, but she didn't expect anything else with how hot the Georgia summer was.

She stepped into the room cautiously, letting her eyes adjust. Penny entered behind her and slapped the light switch on the wall. As soon as the lights flooded the room, Sadie froze.

Martin was lying in his bed under the covers, curled on his side, too still.

"Um, Sadie," Penny said, her words tight and panicked.

Sadie ignored her and took a step closer to the bed. She had to check him, but something about the silence and stillness of the room warned her she wasn't going to like what she found. She pulled the blankets back and pressed her fingers to his neck, but as soon as she touched him, she knew he had been dead for hours. His skin was cold and stiff beneath her fingers. She jerked her hand back like she had been stung.

"Is he…?" Penny trailed off.

Sadie gave a strained nod.

Her friend let out a quiet moan. "Let's get out of here. We can call 911 from the lobby."

"Hold on," Sadie said.

She spotted something on the table next to the bed—the little paper bag from Sunshine Desserts. A cookie sat half-eaten on the wood next to it, but it wasn't one of the ones they had in stock at the motel. Sadie knew that for a fact, since she had helped Hunter with the cookies herself.

"Did he order this cookie yesterday?" she asked.

"What?" her friend asked faintly. "What are you talking about?"

Sadie pointed. "This cookie. Right here. It was in a bag on the front desk. I thought he must have called the lobby to order one to his room and you forgot to give it to him."

"No," her friend said, sounding almost offended. "I wouldn't forget to bring it to him, and no one called in to order a cookie. I'd remember. The only people answering the phone are me and you."

The sick feeling in Sadie's stomach only increased. She slipped her phone out of her pocket and snapped a picture of the cookie.

"What are you doing?" Penny hissed. "We have to get out of here. He's dead, Sadie."

"I know," she said. "He's dead, and this cookie somehow appeared in our lobby with his name on it. I'm the one who gave it to him. What if it was, I don't know, poisoned or something? I need to ask Bailey if it came from her bakery."

"You're as paranoid as he was," Penny said. "The guy probably had a heart attack or something. Heck, maybe he was on drugs. That would explain the paranoia and why he wanted you to hide that lockbox. I bet it's full of drugs, even if he claimed otherwise. Let's get out of here."

They backed out of the room. Sadie paused to lock the door before Penny grabbed her hand and dragged her back to the lobby. She was glad they didn't run into any other guests on the way because she wasn't sure if she would be able to pretend everything was all right.

Penny snatched her cell phone from the front desk as soon as the lobby door shut behind them and dialed 911, her hands shaking. Sadie turned toward the door that led up to her apartment.

"Where are you going?" Penny whispered, covering the receiver with one hand.

"I'm going to put Jasper in his kennel. I'm sure the police will want to see the lockbox, but they're going to have to go up to get it. There's no way I'm touching it again, not with my bare hands. Not without knowing what's in it."

CHAPTER FIVE

"Could be natural causes. Could be something else."

Sheriff Islington adjusted his brimmed hat to keep the sun out of his eyes as he rejoined Sadie and Penny outside of Room Ten. Penny, who had her arms wrapped around herself for comfort despite the heat of the day, scoffed, then looked immediately apologetic.

"Sorry," she said quickly. "It's just… that's not exactly helpful, is it? One of our guests is dead. How are we supposed to know what to do next if you don't even know what happened? Should we close the motel?"

"I don't think that's necessary," the sheriff said. He reached up to stroke his goatee. The tall, lanky man looked like a villain out of a Wild West movie, but Sadie thought he was the decent sort despite his appearance. "There were no disturbances during the night?"

"Nothing that the security cameras alerted me about," Sadie said. "I haven't gone through the footage yet."

"Send it over to the sheriff's department, and I'll have someone get on that," he said. He nodded toward the door. "Lock this back up. The coroner will be here in about half an hour. I don't want anyone disturbing the scene until then."

"What about the cookie?" Sadie asked as she relocked the door. "Someone left it on the front desk for him, but it wasn't me or Penny."

"I'll take it into evidence," he said. "It could be a coincidence. Bailey got a new delivery boy, didn't she? I'll swing by her store after this, see if he ordered it from there."

That was a possibility Sadie hadn't thought of yet. She hadn't seen Hunter stop by again, but she supposed they could have missed him. It had been a busy day and they hadn't had eyes on the lobby every second.

She saw the curtains in Room Six twitch as they walked back toward the lobby and saw Paul look out of them. A moment later, he opened the door.

"Hello, officer," he said, glancing at Sheriff Islington before refocusing on Sadie. "Is there trouble?"

Sadie hesitated, exchanging a glance with Penny. Before they could figure out what to say, Sheriff Islington said, "There's been a fatality in Room Ten. Can I have your name, sir? I'd like to ask you a few questions."

Sadie waited with Penny at a distance while the sheriff asked Paul whether he'd heard anything during the night or if he noticed anything unusual about the guest in Room Ten. Paul hadn't, which didn't surprise Sadie—there were three rooms between his room and the room where Martin had died, and any disturbance loud enough for him to hear probably would have caught the attention of the dogs, too.

"Do you think it was a murder?" he asked when the sheriff finished. "I was doing some reading into the history of this place—"

"No, no, it's nothing like the murders that happened a couple of years ago," Sadie said quickly. "The sheriff thinks the guest died of natural causes, isn't that right?"

Sheriff Islington raised his eyebrows, but nodded. "I won't know for sure until later, but that's my guess.

There's no sign of violence or forced entry. I don't think anyone here needs to be concerned."

"Well, all right. I didn't know about the reputation this place had before I stayed. You really should advertise that somewhere."

Paul retreated back into his room, and she heard the click of the deadbolt engaging. Penny groaned as they continued on their way.

"This is a disaster," she said. "We're two weeks in, and we already have a dead guest."

Sadie held the door open for her friend and the sheriff, then stepped into the lobby with them. The air conditioning was a relief, but it didn't do anything to quell the twisting in her stomach.

"If it really was natural causes, it might not be that bad for the motel's reputation," she said.

"No, it's still going to be bad," Penny said. "The fact that you put him in Room Ten makes it even worse. People are going to start thinking that room is cursed."

"The two of you can argue about this ill-fated venture later," Sheriff Islington said. "I'd like to see that lockbox now."

"I'll take you upstairs," Sadie said.

"I'll keep an eye on the lobby," Penny told them, retreating to sit behind the front desk. "Don't take too long, though. I hate sitting here knowing there's a dead body in one of the rooms."

Sadie unlocked the door that led up to her apartment and made her way up the narrow set of stairs. The sheriff looked around when they reached the living room, curious, but followed her into her bedroom without comment. She was glad. She still hadn't changed the decor or painted, and no matter what she did, the smell of old people and potpourri lingered.

"It's on the top shelf in my closet, all the way to the back," she said. "I have no idea what's in it. He swore it wasn't anything dangerous, but…"

She trailed off, watching as the sheriff put on a pair of thin rubber gloves.

"Considering the state he ended up in, I'm not going to be taking him at his word. Step back."

She backed away to her bedroom door and watched as he carefully removed the lockbox, then set it on her bed.

"Do you have a towel or garbage bag I could put under this in case whatever is inside spills out when I open it?"

She nodded and quickly fetched an old towel from her linen closet. She spread it out on the bed, then retreated again while he put the box on top of it. He examined the lock for a second, then withdrew a slender case from his pocket.

"Are those lock picks?" she asked as he opened it.

He glanced her direction. "Your friend reported that the deceased left behind a mysterious locked box. Now, I don't normally carry these around with me, but it seemed a good opportunity to break them out. Can you back up a little further? I doubt there are explosives in here, but I'd rather not take the risk of harming a civilian."

She backed into the hall and peered around the corner to watch as he fiddled with the lock. When she saw the top click open and nothing bad happened, she inched closer. He opened it and stared inside. She inched even closer, then her breath caught in her throat when she saw what was hidden in the box.

Money. Stacks upon stacks of hundred dollar bills. It explained how he miraculously produced more cash when he came back to ask her to store the box for him.

She felt an intense, selfish stab of regret for telling the sheriff about the locked box, but quickly smothered it. The money wasn't hers, and it very well might have gotten someone killed. No matter how much it might have helped, turning it in was the right thing to do.

It was probably a good thing that she hadn't tried

to snoop in the lock box herself. The decision to turn it over would have been a lot more difficult to make if she knew what it contained.

"Well," the sheriff said, staring down at the money. "Maybe the cause of his death wasn't so natural after all. No one carries around this much cash unless they're planning on doing something illegal with it—or they got it *by* doing something illegal. What did you get yourself involved in, Martin?"

"Did you know him?" she asked as he shut the box with a click.

"Oh, I knew him, all right," Sheriff Islington said. "Martin Gleason grew up here in Greencreek. He left about five years ago, after his divorce turned nasty. I didn't expect to see him again. I definitely didn't expect him to come back here to die."

"He has an ex-wife in town?" Sadie asked, the mention jogging something in her memory. "Who is it?"

"Tiffany Underwood," he said. "You might know her son, Hunter. I heard rumor he's Bailey's new driver."

"He dropped the cookies off yesterday," Sadie said, her mind racing. "Is he Martin's son? I thought he recognized him, but they didn't say anything to each other."

Sheriff Islington shook his head. "Stepson," he said as he picked the box up. "If he was here yesterday, I'll need to speak to him."

"Tiffany was here as well," Sadie said. "I think she recognized his SUV."

He frowned. "Then I'll need to talk to her, too. Forget what I said about natural causes. This stinks of homicide."

CHAPTER SIX

Sadie stood in the doorway and watched Sheriff Islington pull away. Only when he vanished from view did she shut the door and turn back to Penny, who was still sitting behind the front counter, her skin paler than usual.

The coroner had come and gone, and so had their guest in Room One. When the older woman returned to find the county coroner loading a body bag into the back of his transport vehicle, she decided a one night stay was more than enough for her. Now that Martin had checked out as well, that left Paul as their only guest, and Sadie wasn't sure how much longer he would stick around.

"This is bad, Sadie," Penny said. "Really bad."

"I know," Sadie said.

She peered out the window. Martin's vehicle was still there, though the sheriff said someone would show up to tow it away either in the next day or so. Other than her SUV and Penny's red crossover, Paul's car was the only other vehicle in the lot. She turned back to her friend as Penny spoke again.

"He really said he changed his mind about it being from natural causes? We can't have another murder here. It's bad enough with what happened during the open house. But now, with this…"

"Do you think I don't know that?" Sadie groaned and sank down on one of the uncomfortable chairs across from the front counter. "I should have asked him to move on when he tried to get me to rent him a room without seeing his ID."

Penny sighed, her shoulders slumping. "Maybe. Agreeing to hold on to the lockbox for him was a bad idea, too, but I probably would have done the same thing. We can't afford to turn away paying guests."

"We can't afford to have *no* guests, either," Sadie said. "If I'd turned him away, we would have lost one customer. Now, who knows how many we'll lose?"

"I'm trying to make you feel better," her friend said. "What should we do? What if whoever killed Martin comes back?"

"I think they got what they wanted," Sadie said.

"He knew someone was after him. I just thought he was crazy, but obviously I was wrong. If someone did kill him, they wouldn't have a reason to come back, would they?"

"What if they were looking for the lock box?" Penny said. "They might come back for that."

Sadie winced. She hadn't thought of that. "Let's look through the security footage and see if anyone we don't recognize came in right before I found that cookie."

Sadie went back to the kennels to get Jasper, then dragged a chair around behind the front desk, positioning it so she could look over Penny's shoulder and see her laptop screen. Penny logged into their account on the security cameras' website and scrolled down to find the recorded footage. Their cameras didn't record constantly. Instead, they triggered whenever they detected movement.

Sadie used to have the app on her phone set up to notify her whenever any of the cameras sensed a person, but after they opened their doors to guests, she only left the notifications for the kennels and the outdoor runs active. With people coming and going at all hours, she would never get a moment's rest otherwise.

"What time did you see it?" Penny asked.

"I don't remember exactly. It was later in the evening. Maybe around seven. I had just come out of the kennels and had begun cleaning the lobby when I saw it."

Penny frowned and played clips of footage until she found the one of Sadie leaving the lobby with the little paper bag in her hand.

"All right, so we know for sure the cookie was in the lobby by then," she said, recording the time. "When's the last time you know for sure you didn't see the cookie?"

Sadie shrugged, refraining from mentioning that they didn't even know if the cookie was what killed Martin. It was the only lead they had to go on at the moment.

"I have no idea. We were so busy it could have been sitting there for hours and I might not have noticed it. Do you remember seeing it?"

"No, but like you said, we were busy. We know it couldn't have been there before Martin checked in, at least. That was late morning, right?"

Sadie nodded. Penny found the video from when Martin first arrived and recorded the time. It left them with an eight-hour span of time when the cookie could have appeared.

They spent the next hour watching every clip

between those two times. Guests came and went, and a few people used their parking lot to turn around, but there were only two people who stood out to her: Hunter Underwood, and then, a few hours later, his mother, Tiffany. According to the sheriff, they both knew Martin, and Tiffany had even said she recognized his vehicle. She didn't seem to have anything in her hands when she entered the lobby, but she had a big purse that could have been hiding anything.

"Do you think it was her?" Penny asked, pausing the video on Tiffany. "The sheriff said they had a nasty divorce, right? That could be motive for murder."

"Maybe," Sadie said.

"If it wasn't one of them, I don't know who it could be," Penny said. "I mean, there's a few other people who came and went, but why would someone just randomly decide to poison Martin if they didn't know him?"

"Hey, hold on," Sadie said. "Play that clip again."

Penny played the clip of Paul entering the lobby shortly after five that evening. He didn't have anything in his hands, but he did have large pockets on those cargo shorts. She watched as he went into the lobby briefly, then less than a minute later, left again. She didn't remember seeing him in there, but it was possible the lobby was empty at the time. He passed by his room, number Six, and walked all the way down to Room Ten at the end of the row. When he reached the end of the sidewalk, he just stood there, stretching and gazing off down the road as he cracked his neck. He didn't look particularly threatening, but it was enough to make her take note.

"You think it's this guy?" Penny asked, pausing the video. "He looks like someone's dad."

"Well, plenty of people's dads have committed murders," Sadie said. "It's not like he's a good guy just because he's wearing a Hawaiian shirt and sandals with socks."

"I guess we can't count anyone out yet," Penny said. "He *did* show up not long after Martin checked in."

"Will you check the system?" Sadie asked. "I don't remember his last name. I want to look him up."

Two minutes later, Penny had logged out of the security cameras website and had logged onto her social media account, and they were running a search on Paul Anderson.

His social media presence wasn't any more intimidating than his real-life presence was. According to his profile, he worked in finance, he lived in Boston, just like he said, and he had a hairless cat that, judging from his profile, he doted on—plus a girlfriend he seemed to be deeply in love with. There was nothing on his profile to suggest he had a motive to kill Martin.

Sadie knew the money in the lockbox could be enough of a motive all on its own, but how in the world could Paul have known about it? Martin didn't seem like the type to go around bragging about it, not when he went to such lengths to keep the lockbox hidden.

They looked up the Underwoods next. Hunter didn't have much of a social media presence, but his mother, Tiffany, did. She primarily posted photos of herself out to lunch with friends, or photos of her Yorkshire Terrier, Petunia, but the most recent post was one that caught Sadie's eye.

Pouring one out for my ex today. Martin, you got what was coming to you. If this isn't karma, I don't know what is.

"It looks like she knows about his death already," Penny murmured. "And she definitely hated him."

"The good news is the sheriff already thinks she's a person of interest. I'm sure he'll talk to her soon, if he hasn't already. What time is it?"

Penny minimized the browser so they could see the clock. "Just after noon. Why?"

"I'm thinking about running into town. I want to talk to Bailey about that cookie, and I figured I could grab us something for lunch while I'm out."

"You're going to leave me here alone?"

"You have pepper spray," Sadie said. "I'll leave Jasper in here with you. He'll protect you."

Penny looked down at the dog, who was flopped on his side on the floor, his tongue lolling out of his mouth. When he saw them looking at him, his tail thumped once.

"I could be getting mauled by a werewolf, and he wouldn't lift a finger to help me."

"Only because he doesn't have any fingers," Sadie said. "Someone has to be here. It's the middle of the day, we have guests—well, a guest—and there's still a couple of dogs in the boarding kennel. I won't be long. Half an hour, at most."

"Fine," Penny grumbled. "I wish we'd kept that stupid plexiglass up in front of the counter now."

"I told you Walter Bennington must have put it up for a reason," Sadie said as she rose to her feet. "Just don't eat any cookies until I get back, and you'll be fine."

CHAPTER SEVEN

"Nope. No way. I'm not listening to this."

"I'm not accusing you of anything," Sadie said. She was standing at the end of one of the cookie-filled display cases, watching as Bailey, the owner of Sunshine Desserts, scrubbed the glass angrily.

"Are you sure about that?" the other woman asked. "Because to me, it sounds like you're saying you think another one of my employees might be involved in a murder. A murder that happened at *your motel.* Look, I like you, and I like Penny, and I really like that you want to sell my cookies, but it's not my fault that your motel is cursed."

"Our motel isn't cursed," Sadie said. "We've just had some bad luck."

Bailey turned to give her a look. "And what do

you call things that consistently have bad luck, especially of the fatal kind? Cursed."

"Can you just tell me if this is one of your cookies?" Sadie asked. She unlocked her phone and pulled up the picture she had taken of the half-eaten cookie, then held it out to Bailey, who put her cleaning rag down with a sigh and took the phone with her, pinching to zoom in.

"No, that's not one of mine," she said, handing the phone back to Sadie. "It's too small, and it's definitely not a recipe I sell. It looks homemade, probably by an amateur. I can tell the dough was too wet when it was baked."

"Then how did it get into a paper bag from Sunshine Desserts?" she asked, taking her phone back. "And how did it end up at the motel's front desk?"

"I don't know," Bailey said. "But it wasn't me, and it wasn't Hunter. Do you really think this cookie might have killed that guy?"

"I don't have any proof yet, but…yeah, I think it did. Someone dropped a mysterious cookie off in the lobby with Martin Gleason's name written on the bag, and hours later, he's dead. What am I supposed to think?"

Bailey sighed. "The sheriff was in here, asking me

the same thing. He said he's going to rush some tests on the cookie. I'll tell you what I told him: I'm sorry about what happened, but I didn't have anything to do with it. Anyone could have gotten one of those little bags from us. We sell cookies to everyone in town. This doesn't have anything to do with me, or my cookies, or my employees."

"But the guy who died was Hunter's stepfather," Sadie said. "You don't think that's suspicious?"

Bailey put her hands on her hips. "Hunter's twenty-four years old. Martin married his mom when he was nineteen and already living on his own. He might have been Hunter's stepdad, but they hardly knew each other. Plus, from what I heard, his mom came out on top in the divorce. Why would he risk everything to poison a guy he's probably all but forgotten about by now?"

Sadie scowled, but didn't have an answer for that. She didn't know enough about the divorce to say whether Hunter might have had a motive, and she had to admit that he probably wouldn't have had time to sneak the poisoned cookie into the motel. He wouldn't have known Martin was there before he arrived with the cookie delivery, and they hadn't seen him return in any of the security footage.

"Look, I'm sorry this happened," Bailey said.

"But don't blame it on Hunter. I don't want rumors spreading around town, and I can't afford to lose another employee. Now, can I get you anything?"

Sadie was about to say no, but she realized at the last second that she would probably regain some good will from the other woman if she bought something. With their unfortunate lack of guests, they still had plenty of cookies at the motel that she and Penny could enjoy, so she ended up getting one of the almond cookies she knew Sam liked best.

Sadie made sure to tip an extra couple of dollars, and Bailey gave her a grudging farewell as she left. She returned to her SUV, where she sat in the passenger seat while she ordered takeout from the diner across the street: two chicken salad wraps and a large fry to share. Turning the air conditioning up to full blast, she settled down to scroll on social media and check the motel's email while she waited.

When she glanced up from her phone to see Sam walking into the diner, she hurried to unbuckle her seatbelt. She hadn't told him what happened yet and figured that as his landlord, she owed it to him to warn him about the recent murder at the motel. She supposed it hadn't been confirmed to be a murder yet, but she didn't need the sheriff to read her the coroner's report to know that was what it was.

She jogged across the street and let herself into the diner just behind him. He looked around when the door opened, and raised his hand in a silent wave.

She joined him in line and said, "Hey, are you getting lunch?" only to feel dumb when he nodded—of course he was, it was lunchtime, and he was at a restaurant. Rallying, she added, "I'm grabbing a takeout order soon. Mind if we chat while we wait?"

He shook his head and waved at her to go ahead. She glanced at the person in front of them in line—an older woman who seemed engrossed with reading the specials on the board behind the register—and lowered her voice as she asked the next question.

"Have you heard about what happened at the motel?"

He gave her a cautious look and shook his head. Great, she got to be the bearer of bad news. She lowered her voice to a whisper, not wanting the woman in front of them to hear, even though she knew word would eventually spread no matter what she did.

"There's, uh, been another fatality."

He frowned and reached for his phone, typing a message before turning the screen toward her.

Homicide?

"Possibly," she said. "Nothing's certain yet, but I

think someone might have been poisoned. He was staying in Room Ten."

That room is cursed, he typed back. *Are you okay?*

"We're fine. Well, we're pretty freaked out. There's more, but I should probably wait until later to tell you about it." While the murder was going to be common knowledge, she didn't think the lockbox full of money was. "I'm just picking up lunch for me and Penny, then I'm going to head back to the motel. We haven't had a chance to figure out what we're going to do next."

I'm on my way home, too, he typed.

"Really? If you want to eat with us, I'll tell you about the rest of it."

He nodded and tucked his phone away. She took her own phone out to send an update to Penny, then stood in comfortable silence with Sam while they waited for their food.

CHAPTER EIGHT

As soon as Sadie got back to the motel, she hurried into the kennels to check on the dogs and refresh their bowls of water, then brought Jasper back to the lobby with her, where Sam and Penny were already unwrapping their food. Jasper trotted over to Sam, who stopped what he was doing to greet the happy foxhound.

More than anything, Sadie wanted their business to be bursting at the seams with happy guests, both of the human and canine varieties. But for now, that was a pipe dream, and she tried to look at the silver lining —the lack of guests meant that she and Penny had ample time to take a long lunch, and without people coming and going, Jasper could hang out in the lobby with them all day long.

"Thanks for getting lunch," Penny said as Sadie pulled a chair over to join them at the front desk. "Did Bailey say anything?"

"She said she didn't recognize the cookie but swears Hunter couldn't have been involved," Sadie said. "That was about it. I think she's a little miffed that we're blaming her again."

"Well, technically we're blaming Hunter, not her," Penny said. "But I get it. It's not like we're thrilled with this turn of events either."

Sam had carried his notebook in, and wrote with one hand while he ate. *What happened?*

Sadie took a deep breath. "It started when this guy named Martin Gleason came in and asked if he could stay here without showing ID. That was the first red flag. The second was when he asked me to store a mysterious lockbox in my apartment…"

She told him the full story of Martin Gleason's arrival, his paranoia, the cookie she hand delivered to him, and eventually, his death. Guilt gnawed at her as she spoke—she hadn't known it, but if the cookie really was poisoned, then she had unknowingly handed him his murder weapon on a silver platter. Well, in a paper bag.

Thankfully, Sam didn't comment on her mistakes,

even though she had made a lot of them. He simply listened, interested but not judging.

"So, yeah," she finished. "That's about it. We don't know for a fact that the cookie poisoned him—I guess it's possible he had a heart attack or a stroke or something—but with everything else that happened, it doesn't seem very likely."

"Yeah, it'd be too much of a coincidence," Penny said.

Sam snorted, then wrote. *It's already enough of a coincidence that you put him in Room Ten.*

Sadie wrinkled her nose. Room Ten was where all of the other murders had happened. Yes, it was a coincidence, but that didn't mean the room was cursed. She was sure whatever happened to him would have happened regardless of what room he was in. It was just bad luck. That was all.

"It's the money in the lockbox that bothers me the most," Penny said. "I didn't see it myself, but Sadie did, and it sounded like a *lot* of cash. How do you even get that much cash? I'm pretty sure banks don't carry that much on hand, unless you call ahead of time to request it."

"He must have been involved in something illegal or dangerous," Sadie said. "He knew someone was going to come after him. The sheriff said he grew up here in Greencreek. Did you know him, Sam?"

He shook his head. Sadie knew it was a long shot, but it would have been convenient if he did. She sighed and dipped a fry in a little container of ranch dressing, chewing as she thought.

"I think he was a drug dealer," Penny announced.

"I don't know," Sadie replied. "He seemed kinda unprepared. If he was a hardened criminal, he probably would have had a fake ID instead of asking me if he could not show it. Maybe he just… sold an expensive car, or something."

"So why not put the money in a bank?" Penny asked. "If he got it legitimately, it would be the safest place for it."

That was a good point. Sadie shrugged. She couldn't think of a good reason not to put that much cash in the bank if it was obtained legally. She certainly wouldn't want to risk walking around with that much money in cash.

Does anyone else know about the lockbox? Sam wrote.

Sadie shook her head. "No, other than Sheriff Islington, I don't think anyone does. Besides you and Penny, of course. Please don't tell anyone else, it could be important to the case."

My lips are sealed, he wrote.

She let out an amused huff, then sighed. "Sorry, Sam. I feel like we've been nothing but trouble for you since we bought the motel. I really hope the coroner's report shows that Martin had a heart attack and the sheriff can drop the case. I think that would be best case scenario for all of us."

They continued to chat while they ate. Penny was the first one done. As soon as she finished her food, she gathered her trash and rose to her feet.

"I'm going to head back to my room for a little bit," she said. "If any guests arrive, or if the person in Room Six needs anything, let me know and I'll take care of it."

"Yeah, go ahead," Sadie said. It wasn't as if there was anything either of them needed to do at the moment. "We should think about running some more advertisements, but we can figure that out later."

Penny paused to give Jasper a quick pat goodbye, then went outside, leaving Sadie and Sam alone in the lobby. He was almost done with his meal, but she didn't want him to leave right away. It was nice to have someone to talk to, and she missed all of her friends in Lexington. While Penny was her best friend, she needed other people in her life too. Staying cooped up with one other person for days at a time couldn't be healthy for anyone.

She cast about for a conversation topic that would keep Sam engaged. The murder—or the *mysterious death*—was the obvious topic to latch onto, but she was tired of thinking about it. The entire subject filled her with a sense of dread and guilt she couldn't shake, so she decided to broach a topic she had been meaning to bring up for a while instead.

"Hey, how would you feel about teaching me some more sign language?" she asked. "I'd like to learn so we don't have to rely on the notebook all the time."

He looked momentarily surprised, but pleased by her request and moved his sandwich wrapper to the side so he could begin teaching her a couple of signs for basic questions, such as *"How are you doing?"* and *"Can you repeat that?"*

She watched his hands move and tried to mirror the gestures, though it was more difficult than she expected. Spanish had come easily to her, and she even remembered enough to get by if she came across a telenovela while she was switching channels, but sign language was harder. It wasn't just a new language, but an entirely new way of speaking.

They practiced for nearly an hour before Sam

finally gathered his trash and stood up. He had another yard to mow and it was threatening rain. She walked him to the door and waved as he got back into his truck, then returned to the comfortable chair behind the desk and spent a few moments ruffling Jasper's ears before she stood back up with a sigh. She should probably take the dogs on their walks before the rain hit, which meant she should see if Penny was willing to watch the lobby.

The lobby door opened before she made it out from behind the desk. She looked over, expecting to see her friend, but it was Paul Anderson instead. He had a sheepish look on his face, and wouldn't quite look her in the eye as he approached the desk.

"Hi, there," he said in his Boston accent. "I'm glad I caught ya. I have something of a favor to ask."

"What is it?" Sadie asked as she reached down to grab Jasper's collar—he was friendly, but she didn't know if Paul liked dogs, and their reputation was already damaged enough without someone leaving a review complaining about Jasper.

"I had originally asked for the room for three nights," he said. "But I think I'm going to leave tomorrow morning instead of the day after. Would it be possible to pay for only the two nights I'll be using the room, instead of all three?"

"Absolutely," she said. "As long as you check out by eleven tomorrow morning, we'll only charge you for two nights."

He looked grateful. "Thanks. That's a load off my mind."

"I hope your stay has been pleasant," she said.

"Oh, it's been fine. It's nothing personal, but, well…" He rubbed the back of his neck. "I was just in town, and whenever I mentioned where I was staying, I was met with a lot of concern. I have to admit I feel a little misled—from what I heard, the guest who passed away here may not have passed from natural causes after all."

Sadie winced. "I'm sorry. In my defense, the sheriff had originally said he suspected natural causes. We don't have an answer either way yet. Please keep in mind that a lot of what you might have heard in town is speculation."

"I understand, and I wish you the best." He turned toward the door, then paused and turned back toward her. "Forgive me for asking, but I get the feeling business has been tough lately?"

She groaned and flopped back down into office chair, patting Jasper's head idly. "You have no idea. I'm starting to think we made a mistake buying this place."

"Oh, don't say that," he said. "It's got promise. You know, I work with loans, and we offer some very good deals, especially if you can offer collateral. I'd be willing to work with you if you think you're going to need that sort of help."

Sadie hesitated, then shook her head. "Thanks, but we both want to keep from accumulating debt as much as we can. At least this way, if we sell the place, we're not going to be any worse off than we were before we bought it."

"Fair enough," he said. "I'll leave you my business card before I go tomorrow morning, in case you change your mind."

With that, he raised a hand in farewell and stepped out of the lobby. Sadie rose to her feet, her mind replaying his offer. Going into debt seemed like a bad idea to her, but… didn't people usually go in debt when they opened a new business? Maybe they needed to rethink their strategy, because if this kept up, their only other choice was going to be to sell the motel.

CHAPTER NINE

With nothing else to do, Sadie spent the rest of the evening with the dogs. Beth, their weekend regular, dropped off Rosco like usual. She took him and the bulldog on long walks, then spent an hour outside with Jasper, letting him roam the forest off-leash while she walked and thought.

Life had been a constant series of ups and downs ever since they bought the motel. When things were going well, she was happy with their decision. Running a business with her best friend—and not just any business but her dream business—was something few people were lucky enough to do. On the other hand, constantly being on the edge of financial ruin and living somewhere that was known around town as the murder motel, wasn't exactly…fun. She and

Penny had both known this wouldn't be easy, but they hadn't expected to be signing up for murder and mayhem.

The next day was Saturday, which meant Tiffany Underwood was supposed to bring her yorkie, Petunia, for an overnight stay. A single overnight wasn't much, but at least it was something, and Sadie hoped against hope Petunia would become a new regular client. It sounded like Tiffany hadn't felt comfortable enough to travel for a long time, so if Petunia's stay went well, she might want to make up for lost time. At the very least, she had a two-week-long cruise coming up, which would be a significant amount of income for them.

That meant things had to go well. On Saturday morning, after she finished her usual chores, she took extra time to make sure the first kennel was absolutely perfect. She even went so far as to rake the pea stones in the run outside and double and triple check that there were no gaps that the little dog could possibly slip through.

With how small Petunia was, she didn't think she would give the dog access to the outdoor run unsupervised. The kennel runs didn't have tops, which was fine for the larger dogs since they weren't in any danger from hawks or owls, but the little yorkie would be at risk. Petunia would have to be supervised whenever she went outside. She lowered the barrier between the indoor and outdoor runs, then swept the lobby and checked in with Penny to see whether Paul had checked out yet.

"Not yet," her friend said. She was busy on her laptop, trying to design a new advertisement to run online. "Maybe he changed his mind. If he stays past eleven, we're charging him."

"I think we should let it go if he's only a few minutes late," Sadie said. "A great review could be worth more than an extra night's stay."

Penny wrinkled her nose but didn't argue. Without much else to do, she helped Penny design the ad until the lobby door opened. Sadie looked up, expecting either Paul or Tiffany, but instead of either of them, Hunter walked in. He was wearing a shirt with the Sunshine Desserts logo, and a backwards ball cap that reminded her of Bailey's last delivery driver.

"Hey," he said, fanning himself as the lobby door swung shut behind him "Hot day out today. The air conditioning in here feels amazing."

"Yeah, we're lucky to have it," Sadie said. "How can I help you? We're not expecting another cookie delivery, are we?"

"No, Bailey asked me to see if you were ready to pay that invoice I left with you the other day."

"Shoot," Sadie muttered. "I completely forgot about that. Let me go get the business checkbook, and I'll pay it right away."

Their business account was all but empty, but they could afford to pay for the cookies. She fetched the checkbook, found the invoice where she had stored it under the register, and began to fill out the check. It was something she was unpracticed in— he didn't think she had paid for anything with a handwritten check before in her life before they bought the motel —and Penny snickered when she messed up writing down the amount and had to start over.

"Sorry," she muttered. "Thanks for waiting."

"No problem at all," Hunter said.

She watched him out of the corner of her eye as Penny took over the check writing. He took a casual seat in one of their waiting chairs, directly under the air conditioning vent, seemingly unconcerned that his stepdad had died just a few doors down.

"I want to say sorry for your loss," she said.

He looked up, confused. "Huh?"

"Martin Gleason. The sheriff mentioned he was your stepdad?"

He snorted. "Oh, him. I mean, I barely knew the

guy and he was a jerk. Like, it's sad he's dead and everything, but he cheated on my mom so it's hard to care much."

"Oh, I didn't know," Sadie said. "I'm sorry. That must have been hard for her."

He shrugged. "Yeah, I mean, she was pretty upset, but in the end, it worked out okay. Like I said, he was a jerk anyway, and he made her sign a prenup where she wouldn't get anything if they divorced…with an exception for infidelity or abuse. He invalidated his own prenup, and she got pretty much everything in the divorce. I think he spent most of what she didn't take on lawyers, trying to get the judge to change his mind. In the end, she bought him out of both the business and the house and now she's living her best life."

Penny spoke up for the first time. "He can't have been happy about that. Do you think he came back to cause trouble for her?"

Hunter snorted. "The jerk left town with nothing to his name. I think he was too embarrassed to stick around—I heard he moved all the way to Boston, which tells me he wanted nothing to do with this place. I couldn't tell you why he came back, but it's kind of ironic that he had a heart attack the same night he got here. It's karma, if you ask me."

"Did he have a heart attack?" Sadie asked,

exchanging a look with Penny. "The sheriff didn't seem sure when we talked to him."

"Well, he said he didn't know for sure, but what else could it be?" Hunter said. "The guy was a loser, he wasn't involved in anything interesting enough to rate being murdered. The sheriff said foul play was suspected when he talked to me, but I think he's just being paranoid because of everything else that happened at this motel. No offense."

"None taken," Sadie said. "Trust me, we know how bad it looks."

"Yeah, sorry about that. Martin always messes things up for everyone."

"You don't have any idea why he came back here?" Sadie said. "Would he have tried to talk to your mom?"

Hunter snorted. "Heck no, he didn't want anything to do with her. She took him to the cleaners in the divorce, and he had to have known she would make his life harder if he ever came back. He must have been here for some other reason, but I've got no idea what it was. Like I said, we were never close. I haven't spoken to him since before the divorce."

Finally finished writing the check, Penny ripped it out of the checkbook and handed it over to him.

"Here you go," she said. "That should cover us for

this week's delivery. Tell Bailey we'll call before the next one. We haven't had many guests this week, so we might not need as many cookies as usual next week."

"Fair enough," Hunter said, rising to his feet.

"Oh, wait," Sadie said before he left. "Is your mom still planning on stopping by with Petunia later?"

"I think so," he said. "She said she was when she called yesterday. She was a little nervous about it, but she's determined to give it a try. I'll see you around."

He raised his hand in a mock salute and stepped through the lobby door, leaving Sadie with a lot to think about. If what Hunter said was true, then what motive did Tiffany have to kill Martin? She had already gotten everything she wanted out of him. If anything, Martin was the one with a motive to kill her.

CHAPTER TEN

Sadie wanted to spend some time with the dogs while she waited for Tiffany to arrive with Petunia, but Penny had a video call scheduled with her parents, and she had agreed to keep an eye on the lobby until she was done. They couldn't leave it empty, not when they knew Paul wanted to check out early.

Sadie wanted to be there to say goodbye to him, and maybe to talk to him about the loans he could offer. She wasn't going to accept anything, not without talking to Penny first, but she knew it was worth thinking about.

She entertained herself on Penny's computer while she waited. She knew she should have been looking for advertisement and marketing opportunities, but she spent most of her time browsing photos of other motels online. They couldn't afford any of the renovations they wanted to do, but she liked to look and imagine the future.

Their rooms were decent, if basic, so for now, their next priority was the exterior of the motel. She was sure Sam would agree to do the landscaping, especially once they were able to pay him properly, but the building itself needed to be repainted, and they could use some new windows, and frankly, a new roof as well.

She glanced at the clock as she browsed. It was getting closer to eleven, and still no Paul. She stood by what she had said to Penny—if he turned up a few minutes late, it would be worth letting him go without charging him for another night. She wasn't sure what she would do if he checked out hours late and still wanted them to only charge him for two nights. They really could use the money, but it wasn't as if they needed the room for someone else.

Bored, she logged into the security camera application to check on the dogs. Each indoor kennel had its own camera, so she could see that Jasper was chewing on a plastic bone, the bulldog was snoring on his bed. Roscoe wasn't in his kennel, so she switched to the camera that looked over the outdoor runs, where she could see him nosing through the pea stones.

Satisfied that all of the dogs were happy and healthy, she switched to the camera that looked out over the lobby door. Paul's vehicle was still parked in the parking lot, which meant he hadn't done a hands-free check out by sneakily dropping his key in the drop box. Martin's vehicle was still in the lot as well. The sheriff had said the wrecker was supposed to tow it today at the latest, but it was a weekend, so she wasn't sure whether they would actually show up. She frowned and zoomed in on the image, but the cameras were the cheapest they could get, and zooming in just made the screen blurrier. She almost thought it looked like one of the windows on Martin's vehicle was broken.

She pushed the chair back from the desk and was about to stand up to go check on it when, on the screen, she saw a sleek crossover pull into the parking lot. It was now just a few minutes before eleven, which was when Tiffany was supposed to drop Petunia off. That had to be her.

Suddenly nervous, Sadie rose to her feet and looked around the lobby to make sure nothing was out of place. She needed this to go well. Beth and Rosco were lovely clients, but they needed more regulars if they were going to be successful. She realized at the last minute that it would probably be a little strange if she was standing in front of the lobby door with a smile on her face when Tiffany came in, so she forced herself to sit back down behind the desk and tried to look busy on the computer.

She waited a second to look up when the lobby door opened, not wanting to appear too eager. Sure enough, it was Tiffany, carrying a tiny Yorkshire Terrier in her arms, along with her large purse and a zippered tote bag, the latter of which had yorkies printed all over it.

"Hi," Sadie said. "Welcome back. Is this little sweetheart Petunia?"

"Yes, this is my baby," Tiffany said as she carried the little dog over to the front desk. "I'm not sure if this was a good idea. She's terrified. I can feel her shaking already."

The little dog did look frightened. Her soft brown eyes were so wide, Sadie could see the whites of them, and she was quivering in her owner's arms.

"Why don't you put her down on the floor and let her explore a little?" Sadie said. "There's a bowl of water in case she's thirsty, and she's welcome to help herself to Jasper's toys if she wants to. I'll just need her vet records to finish checking her in."

Tiffany carefully lowered the dog to the floor, keeping hold of one end of the yorkie's leash, which was so thin it was practically a string. The dog stood huddled at her feet for a few seconds before she began to sniff the ground cautiously. Lowering the tote bag to the floor, Tiffany put her purse on the front desk and opened it to bring out a folded piece of paper, which she handed over to Sadie.

Sadie scanned it into the computer to save it in their records, then peeked over the counter at Petunia. "How's she doing now?"

"I think she's beginning to settle down a little," Tiffany said, though she still sounded worried.

Sadie wanted to put her at ease, so she said, "It's normal for dogs to be anxious during their first time boarding somewhere new. It's a new place with a lot of strange smells. They usually calm down pretty quickly once they settle in. Do you want to say goodbye to her before I bring her back to the kennel?"

"I was hoping I could walk back with her," Tiffany said. "I want to make sure she's comfortable before I leave."

"All right, we can do that," Sadie said. "Right this way. I have her in the very first kennel. We'll get everything set up for her, and then once you leave, I'll give her some time to settle in. She'll get a walk later this evening, right before dinner."

Tiffany stooped to scoop up her dog and the tote bag again, then followed Sadie through the laundry room and into the kennel area, where the other dogs greeted them with excited barking. Sadie stood back while Tiffany unpacked Petunia's tote bag. She brought out a fluffy bed and five different stuffed toys, then handed the rest off to Sadie: more cans of food than the tiny dog could possibly eat during a one-night stay and a variety of treats.

Sadie put the food items on the metal shelf opposite the kennels, where she kept all the dogs' food on labeled shelves, then stood by quietly while Tiffany kissed the yorkie on top of the head and smoothed her fur gently.

"I'll see you tomorrow, sweetie. You be good for Sadie, okay? Mama will be back. I'm not abandoning you."

She gently lowered the tiny dog into her bed, then shut the kennel door and reached a hand up to wipe her eyes. "Sorry," she said. "I know I'm being ridiculous. It's one night and I know she'll be okay. I just can't stop thinking about how scared and confused she'll be. My ex tried to get rid of her back when we were still married, and I'm worried she's traumatized by that."

"She will be a little nervous," Sadie said, not wanting to lie to the other woman. "That's normal. Once she's stayed here a few times and she knows you're coming back, she'll start getting more and more comfortable. One day, she might even get excited about visiting like Rosco in the second kennel from the end, does. He comes every weekend, and he loves it. She'll get to see the other dogs go in and out, and she'll get a nice long walk every day. Whenever I have a spare second, I'll swing by the kennel and give her some attention, and I'll send you an update this evening if you'd like—one in the morning, too."

"Thanks," Tiffany said. "I appreciate you being so understanding. I'd like to pay now so I don't have to worry about it when I pick her up tomorrow, if that's all right."

"Of course," Sadie said.

Tiffany crouched down to say goodbye to Petunia one last time before following her back through the laundry room and out into the lobby, where they walked over to the front desk. Sadie paused partway across the room when something caught her eye.

Her apartment door was cracked open, just a hair. The sight sent a jolt of alarm through her, because she knew for a fact she had locked her apartment when she came down that morning.

"Is something wrong?" Tiffany asked.

"I'm not sure," Sadie said hesitantly, her mind racing. Who could have done it? Penny had a key, but she had no idea what her friend would have wanted in her apartment, or why she would have unlocked the door without saying something first. "I need to go check on something. I'll be right back."

CHAPTER ELEVEN

Her heart in her throat, Sadie slowly made her way up the stairs, knowing them well enough by now to avoid the steps that were most likely to creak. She eased the door at the top open and felt another spike of alarm. Her living room light was on, and she always turned the lights off when she left a room—something that had been drilled into her by frugal parents, and which was even more important now that each bill was a struggle to pay.

Her eyes flicked to her coffee table where her purse sat. The bag held her pepper spray, which she desperately needed in her hands before she searched the rest of the apartment. She inched into the room and carefully made her way across the old carpet to the coffee table, where she rifled through her purse.

She heard a long, low creak come from behind her just as her fingers closed around the canister. She spun around, raising it in front of her just as Paul Anderson stepped out of her bedroom.

"Whoa," he said, raising his hands, palms up. "You can put that down. I'm not going to hurt you."

"I'm not putting it down," Sadie said. "What are you doing in here?"

"That's fair. I probably wouldn't lower my only weapon if I found someone snooping around my apartment, either," he said. "I'm not stealing anything. You can check my pockets if you want. I didn't even bring any weapons up with me. I don't have anything on me except a set of lockpicks and my wallet, which I'm going to take out of my pocket right now."

Moving slowly, he took a slender packet and a leather wallet out of his pocket, crouching to lower the items to the floor. He patted his pockets to show her they were empty, and then straightened up.

She relaxed slightly but kept the pepper spray aimed at his face. "All right, so you're not armed," she said. "What are you doing in here? Why did you break in?"

"I'm looking for something that belongs to my

employer," he said. "I believe one of your guests had it with him when he checked in."

She didn't have to be a genius to make the connection. "You're talking about the lockbox Martin Gleason had?"

He nodded, looking validated rather than surprised. "When I didn't find it in his room, I suspected he might have asked you to keep an eye on it. It's not the lockbox I'm after, but rather what's in it. I'm guessing you opened it? I know it's a lot of money, but it's not yours to keep. I'm going to need it back. If you hand it over without causing any trouble, I can give you a finder's fee for it. Otherwise, I'm going to have to get the law involved."

"I don't have it," Sadie said. "You're right. He did ask me to look after it, but I didn't know about the cash, and I turned it into the police after he died." She paused, then added a little defensively, "I would have turned it in even if I knew what was in it."

For the first time, she saw Paul's composure slip as he cursed. "You gave it to the police?" he said. "That's going to be a pain to get back. My employer is not going to be happy."

"You said you work with loans, right?" she said. "I'm guessing they aren't the strictly legal kind."

"I do those, too," he said. "But you're right. My employer does some under-the-table type loans for people who wouldn't otherwise be able to get them. Good old Martin pulled a fast one on us. You see, he used his house as collateral for the loan, only for us to find out that he lost the house in his divorce. As soon as we put the pieces together, we knew he was going to take the money and run. By the time we figured it out, he was already gone. My boss sent me to get the money back from him. I had to follow him from Boston, but they always go home eventually. I knew he'd be coming back here."

"Sadie?" The apartment door creaked as someone pushed it open. Sadie turned to see Tiffany peering around the doorframe. Her eyes were wide as she stared first at the pepper spray and then at Paul. "What's going on? I heard voices, and you sounded upset. Do you need me to call the police?"

"Yes, I think you'd better," Sadie said at the same time Paul said, "No, that won't be necessary."

They stared at each other for a moment.

"You broke into my apartment," she said slowly. "Why would I not call the police?"

"I didn't break anything, technically, and I only entered the premises to recover stolen property. I don't really think that's worth involving the law over, do you?"

"Yes, I do," she said. "I don't care why you broke in. You could have started by asking me if I had the lockbox."

"Yes, I probably could have," he said. "But, you see, I suspected that if you came across the money, you might have decided to keep it. Completely understandable, of course—I think most people would have done so—but that meant you probably wouldn't be very eager to hand it over if I asked, even if I asked nicely. And if you knew I was looking for it, you might have taken steps to hide it better than you would otherwise."

"Then you should have called the police," Sadie said. "You broke into Martin's vehicle, too, didn't you? I thought I saw a broken window on the security camera."

"That was an unfortunate accident," Paul said. "I was trying to jimmy the window. It already had a crack, and I went a little too far and shattered it. In the interest of full disclosure, I broke into his motel room earlier this morning. I replaced the police tape, so they shouldn't notice anything is amiss, and I wore gloves while I did it. I touched absolutely nothing but what I had to to ensure the lockbox wasn't there."

"Yes, Tiffany, please call the police," Sadie said, not taking her eyes off of him.

She heard an electronic tone as Tiffany began to dial the number. Paul tried to convince them to drop the matter one last time.

"Please, wait. This is going to complicate everything. I still need to get that money back for my boss—and I didn't damage or take anything of yours. Can't we work something out? I'm willing to pay for your silence if I have to."

"I'm afraid not," Sadie said. "It's not just the breaking and entering. You *killed* someone. I'm not going to let you get away with that, not for any amount of money."

"What?" Paul asked. He looked so genuinely confused that for a second she faltered.

"You killed Martin," she said. "That's what happened, isn't it? You came up here to get the money back and to teach him a lesson."

"I didn't touch the man," Paul said. "He never even knew I was here, and he didn't know me from Adam. I thought you said he died of natural causes. I heard the rumors in town, but I thought those were just rumors. I used them as a convenient excuse to leave a night early since I didn't want to stick around once I found the lock box. I knew you'd see me breaking into the room or the vehicle on the security cameras the next time you reviewed the footage."

"You didn't leave the cookie for him?" Sadie asked. He seemed so genuinely confused that it was hard not to believe him.

"A cookie? Why would I leave the man a cookie?"

"I think that's what killed him," she said. "Poison, of some sort."

Paul looked at her like she had two heads. "If I was here to 'teach him a lesson' or whatever idea you have in your head from watching too many mafia movies, poison isn't how I'd do it. No one gets taught a lesson through poison. No, I'd have used a gun or a knife—something that would make an impact on the next person who thinks they can cheat my employer. Poison is a woman's method of killing."

Sadie stared at him for a second longer, then turned her head to look at Tiffany, who had frozen with the phone still clutched in her hands.

CHAPTER TWELVE

Sadie stared at Tiffany. Tiffany stared back, her eyes widening incrementally as she looked from Paul, then back to Sadie again.

It wasn't Paul's statement alone that made Sadie feel like her brain was glitching. It was everything, the small things and the big things combined. The fact that Tiffany was Martin's ex-wife. The timing of her visit the day before Martin died. Despite claiming that he didn't know his stepfather that well, Hunter had to have recognized him when they ran into each other in the lobby, and he would have had ample opportunity to tell his mother about it when he called to suggest that she try boarding Petunia there.

She visited hours later, which would have given her plenty of time to bake a poisoned cookie, and just like Bailey said, anyone in town could easily obtain one of the little paper bags that Sunshine Desserts used. Especially Tiffany, whose son worked for Bailey.

She had opportunity. The only problem was, Sadie didn't know if she had the motive. Yes, Martin had cheated on her, but it sounded like Tiffany had already had her revenge in court.

Her social media profile showed that she had an active social life with her friends, a dog she loved, and she had a son she was close to. Why would she risk all of that to get revenge on someone who had already paid for what he did, and then some?

In the next second, the answer came to Sadie. What was it Tiffany had said? That he tried to get rid of Petunia? To someone who loved their dog as much as Tiffany loved Petunia, that might be even more unforgivable than infidelity.

"What?" Tiffany asked after long seconds ticked by. "What are you looking at me like that for?"

"Yeah, I feel like I'm missing something," Paul said.

"'Poison's woman's work,'" Sadie said, quoting him. "Tiffany was Martin's ex-wife. She was here the day before he died."

Tiffany took a step back, clutching the phone to

her chest. "What are you saying? If you're going to accuse me of something, spit it out."

"What did Martin do to Petunia?" Sadie asked. Tiffany looked put off-balance by the sudden change in subject.

"He took her to the pound," she said, her voice cracking. "That's why I'm so hesitant to leave her anywhere. I can't stop seeing her little, scared face in the kennel at the pound. Martin hated her. He hated how I doted on her. One day, I came home and she wasn't there. He said she'd gotten outside and he couldn't find her anywhere. I panicked, and I couldn't stop sobbing. I posted her picture everywhere, and I called every vet clinic and shelter in the area. I ended up driving all the way to Atlanta and looking through each shelter in person. I ended up finding her at a municipal shelter. When I asked who brought her in, the woman at the desk gave me Martin's name—he had to leave a copy of his ID when he dropped her off as a 'stray.' I knew then that I wanted to leave him, and I was already in talks with my lawyer about how to handle the divorce when I found out Martin was cheating on me. It was a moment of pure serendipity. It meant I could leave him without losing everything."

Tiffany looked livid when she finished, and Sadie couldn't say she blamed her. If her ex dropped Jasper off at a pound, she didn't think she would ever be able to forgive him.

The story fit in with everything else perfectly. Martin had made enemies in his life—more than one, considering the fact that Paul had chased him halfway across the country to retrieve stolen money from him—but the most dangerous enemy he had ever made was his ex-wife.

Sadie lowered the pepper spray, turning away from Paul so she could face Tiffany fully. "You're the one who left him the cookie, aren't you? You weren't done getting revenge on him."

"Revenge?" Tiffany said, surprised. "I was protecting Petunia. When Hunter said he was back in town, I knew it could only be for one reason. I knew he wanted to get back at me for winning in court, and I knew Petunia was going to be his target. I did what I had to, to keep my precious girl safe. I had eye surgery a few years ago, and since then I've kept eye drops on hand. I put everything I had into that cookie dough. I read online a while ago that eyedrops were toxic if consumed, and it turns out the website was right about that."

Paul let out a low whistle. "Well, it doesn't make up for losing that money, but at least this was an entertaining trip. Can we agree that if you're going to call the police on anyone, it's the lady who killed someone and not me?"

Sadie glanced at Paul and decided to relent, mainly because she realized that being alone in a room with two people who didn't want her to call the police was a bad idea. "If you stick around to talk to the sheriff and tell him what Tiffany said, I won't press charges. But you're going to be banned from the premises after this. Forever."

"Fair enough," he said.

"No, wait," Tiffany said. "You can't do that. You can't turn me in—what I did was justified. What's going to happen to Petunia if I go to prison?"

"We'll take care of her here at the kennel until we figure something out," Sadie promised. "If Hunter is open to taking her, he can have her. Otherwise, I'll help her find a good home. I promise. I know how much you love her and how much she loves you. You're going to have to answer for what you did to Martin, but I'll give you my word that Petunia won't suffer for it."

Whatever Tiffany did, it wasn't Petunia's fault, and the little yorkie deserved a loving home despite her owner's crimes.

EPILOGUE

"Are you sure you don't want to keep her?" Penny asked.

It was a week later, and they were both in Sadie's apartment. A movie was playing on the TV, but neither of them was paying attention to it. Petunia, who was nestled in the blankets on the couch between them, was the center of their focus, as she had been ever since her owner's arrest. True to her word, Sadie was caring for the little dog like her own. Petunia had been frightened the first few days, but she quickly warmed up, especially once Sadie began bringing her up to her apartment in the evenings. She loved cuddling on the couch with her while she watched TV and was even beginning to accept Jasper's presence. The big foxhound was curious about her and kept bringing her his favorite stuffed animal—an elephant that was twice the yorkie's size.

"If she didn't have anywhere else to go, I might be tempted, but Hunter says he wants to take her. He just has to arrange things with his landlord and roommate first," Sadie said. "He's upset about what his mother did, but he still loves her, and I think he'll take good care of her. He can bring Tiffany updates when he visits her in prison, and Petunia's familiar with him. Besides, I told him we'd give him a discount on boarding services in the future, so we'll probably be seeing more of her."

"She's just so tiny and precious," Penny said. "She makes me want a dog of my own. I know I can't afford one right now, but one day…" She trailed off and sighed. "At this rate, it's going to be a long time before I can even afford to upgrade my phone, let alone care for a living animal."

"Things are looking up a little," Sadie said, grasping for something optimistic to say. "We just had that family make a reservation for two rooms for a whole week, and I'm going to host my first training class in two weeks. Plus, Rosco's still staying every weekend. Oh, and Melody said she might want to board Cleo here sometime."

"Well, I hope the training classes are popular,

because we need *something* to go right," Penny said. "Sorry for being a downer. I think it's starting to get to me. We both put everything we had into this, and I'm terrified it was the wrong decision."

"We both knew it was a risk," Sadie said. "But I'm not giving up on us yet. We can make this work. I know we can."

Printed in Dunstable, United Kingdom